GREAT GREEK MYTHS

Contents

Written by Diane Redmond

Illustrated by Julian Mosedale

The Labours of Herakles

Part 1

Herakles was the strongest and mightiest of all the Greek heroes. His mother was mortal, a beautiful woman whom Zeus fell madly in love with. When Hera, Zeus's wife, heard about his new girlfriend she was furious.

"If that mortal woman has your baby, I'll strangle it, in its own cradle!" Hera threatened.

The mortal woman *did* have a baby, Zeus's son, and Hera tracked it down and put two poisonous snakes in its cradle. But baby Herakles grabbed the wriggling snakes in his little fat fists and strangled them. Hera was so impressed by his strength that she decided to let the baby live – at least for a bit longer.

Every year that passed, Herakles grew bigger, stronger and more powerful. The finest athletes in Greece taught him to run and wrestle, and famous warriors taught him to throw the javelin and fight with clubs and swords.

"He's extraordinary," they all said. "Superman – a phenomenon!"

Because he knew he'd been blessed by the gods, Herakles wanted to use his strength to help people. He went to visit the oracle at Delphi and there the wise man spoke to him.

"You must do good," said the oracle, in a low whispering voice.

"How?" asked Herakles.

"Go to Mycenae and live with King Eurystheus. He will tell you what to do."

And that's how the labours of Herakles began.

Herakles's first labour was to kill the lion
of Nemea.

"To prove you've killed it, take the skin off its
back, and bring the skin to me," King Eurystheus
commanded.

Herakles shrugged – killing a lion was no
problem for a strong man like him.

"This is no ordinary lion," warned the king.
"No weapon, so far, has ever been sharp enough to
cut its skin."

"I'll think of something," said Herakles, and
set off with his spear, sword, club and a thick
rope net.

He reached Nemea after many days travelling,
and asked the locals where the famous man-eating
lion lived.

"L-l-l-lion!" they cried. "You can't go near that
monster. It's eaten four babies and a donkey
this week."

"Somebody's got to kill it," said Herakles bravely.

The locals nodded; they didn't mind who killed it
– as long as it wasn't them.

"The lion lives over there," they said, "in a den
knee-deep in bones and skin."

"Thanks," said Herakles. "See you later."

"You'll be lucky," whispered the locals, and they ran home and hid under their beds.

As Herakles walked up the hills, he tripped over bones of all sizes – big bones, little bones, shin bones, backbones, even head bones. He didn't have to look far for the cave – he could smell it a mile away.

Meanwhile, the Nemean lion could smell Herakles. "Yum, yum! Man for supper," he slurped, and went out to meet him.

Herakles couldn't believe the size of the lion – it was huge! As big as a horse, with a flaming mane and eyes that blazed fire. If he hadn't been such a hero, Herakles would have turned tail and run for his life, but instead he grabbed his spear and took aim.

The lion sprang forwards and Herakles hurled the spear straight at him. Z-I-P! The spear hit the lion, but instead of cutting into its skin, the arrowhead shattered and the spear bounced into the bushes. The lion tossed his mane and snarled.

"You don't frighten me, Goldilocks!" laughed Herakles, and pulling out his sword he charged at the lion. Herakles stabbed the sword into the lion's chest, but to his astonishment nothing happened. The lion's skin didn't bleed or break but the sword split clean in two.

Herakles was left with only his club. Gripping the club tightly in both hands, he whacked it in the lion's mouth, but the lion hardly noticed it. He yawned and stretched, then walked off into his den. Herakles was puzzled.

"A bash like that should have knocked his socks off! I need more than strength to kill this monster. I need wisdom too." He fell to his knees and prayed to Pallas Athene, the goddess of wisdom. "Sweet Goddess, guide me, tell me what to do."

Athene heard his prayers and answered them. "Brave Herakles, take your net and cover the lion's cave, then creep inside and kill the beast with your bare hands."

Herakles gulped in fear but he never doubted the words of the goddess – he did exactly what she had told him to do.

He fixed his net across the den, crept in through another entrance and tracked the Nemean lion through the dark, stinking passageways. Finally Herakles cornered the lion. The lion snarled, "GRRRRRRR!"

Herakles wasn't scared. He grabbed the lion by the throat, pressing his fingers tighter and tighter. The lion scratched and clawed, but Herakles kept on squeezing and squeezing until every bit of breath had left the lion's body. Finally it was still – dead still.

"Now to get the skin off its back," said Herakles. "But how, when there isn't a weapon sharp enough to cut through its skin?"

Again, Athene, the goddess of wisdom, helped him.

"Use the lion's claw," she whispered.

"Thank you, Goddess!" prayed Herakles, and chopped off one of the lion's huge claws. It cut through the skin like butter. Wrapping the lion's skin round his body, Herakles returned to Mycenae, very pleased with himself.

But King Eurystheus didn't spend too long congratulating him.

"Off you go on your second labour, and take that stinking Nemean lion's skin with you!" he said. "This time I want you to kill the hydra."

Even though the hydra was a nine-headed, man-eating monster, brave Herakles didn't bat an eyelid. He set off for the coastland near Argos where the hydra lived. Luckily he took his wise servant, Iolaus, with him, otherwise he might never have come back.

Among the trees by the sea, they heard the loud hissing and gurgling of the hydra.

Suddenly the monster sprang out on them with its nine tongues spitting and its 18 eyes blazing.

"DIE!" screamed Herakles as, with all his strength, he struck the hydra and whacked off one of its heads.

"One down, eight to go," thought Herakles. But no such luck!

The minute the dead head touched the ground, another one grew. Taking a deep breath, Herakles ran at the hydra. He chopped off three heads in as many seconds, but they all grew back immediately.

On Mount Olympus, Hera laughed with wicked pleasure.

"I've waited a long time to see you die, Herakles. Now I'm going to have some fun watching you squirm."

At Hera's command, two giant crabs with claws came scuttling across the sand and grabbed Herakles by the ankles, but even then he didn't panic. Taking up his club he smashed each of the crabs on their shells. His strength was so great that the crabs' skulls popped wide open and their brains fell out.

Iolaus, who'd been watching the fight, suddenly had a brainwave.

"If you chop off the hydra's heads, I can singe the ends with a burning log," he called to his master.

So Herakles faced the hydra with Iolaus opposite him holding on to a burning torch.

ZAP! ZAP! ZAP! ZAP! went Herakles's sword. Heads fell in all directions, but before they could grow again, Iolaus singed each bleeding stump with his red-hot torch. Finally, there was only one head left. Herakles clubbed it to jelly and then buried it in the sand.

He took the hydra's body back to Mycenae, but King Eurystheus was not pleased.

"You cheated!" he cried.

"CHEATED!" gasped Herakles. "What did I do wrong?"

"You shouldn't have let your servant help you," said the king. "That wasn't part of the deal."

"By the pillars of Herakles, if Iolaus hadn't helped me, I wouldn't be here to tell the tale!" Herakles pointed out.

"Your next task will be even harder," said King Eurystheus. "You must clean out the stables of King Augeas!"

Herakles sighed heavily. King Augeas lived in Elis, *another* marathon journey to the ends of the earth. He owned a thousand cattle, which were kept in huge stables that had never, *ever* been cleaned out and were two metres deep in dung. The air stank, the island stank, the people stank – and so did King Augeas!

"The filth from the stables is causing sickness and disease," said Eurystheus. "It's up to you to clean them, Herakles."

It took nearly a year to reach Elis, but Herakles had his servant, Iolaus, to keep him company on the way. King Augeas was delighted to see them both, and was thrilled by Herakles's offer.

"I've come to clean out your stables – in a day," he said.

"Unless your day has a thousand hours, you'll never do it," laughed Augeas. "The muck's two metres deep."

"I know," sniffed Herakles. "I can smell it from here."

"Bit pongy, isn't it?" agreed Augeas, who was far too lazy to clean up the stables himself.

"If I manage the job, will you give me a piece of the land that I clear?" asked Herakles.

"Certainly," agreed Augeas. "Take whatever you want."

Herakles and Iolaus set off for the stables, behind which ran two huge rivers. Herakles lifted boulders as big as elephants, blocked both rivers with the boulders, and then re-directed their flow towards the smelly stables.

"This should shift that mountain of muck," he said, with a smile.

Standing on a high cliff, he and Iolaus watched the teeming waters of the rivers join together and thunder downhill. They rushed through the stables, sweeping away the dung that had been piling up for 20 years. W-H-O-O-O-S-H! it went, straight out to the sea.

King Augeas inspected his sparkling clean stables and readily agreed that Herakles had done a marvellous job.

"Take your land, hero," he said, "and welcome."

Herakles chose a fine stretch of land, which has been used, by the Greeks, from that day to this for the site of their Olympic Games.

When he returned to Mycenae, King Eurystheus was ready and waiting with the next task.

"Your fourth labour is to capture the fire-breathing Cretan bull, the minotaur," he said.

Herakles yawned. "I've been round the world twice and just mucked out a stable two metres deep in dung! Do you think I could have a meal and a nice hot bath?" he asked.

The miserable king shook his head.

"Don't start complaining or I shall have a few words to say to Zeus about you," he threatened.

"Sorry," said Herakles, who knew that even a hero has to keep his mouth shut sometimes.

Luckily Crete wasn't too far away and Herakles, with Iolaus, went straight to the city of Knossos and spoke to King Minos.

"We've come to capture the Cretan bull," said Herakles.

Minos was so terrified of the minotaur, he hadn't been out of his palace for years.

"Nobody can catch that monster," he said.

"I can if you tell me where he lives," Herakles promised.

"The minotaur lives outside the city walls," the king replied.

"At least this beast has no magical powers," said Iolaus as they walked around the city walls, looking for the bull.

"That's a relief," said Herakles, but when he saw the size of the bull, his eyes nearly popped out of his head – it was gigantic!

The beast threw back its head and breathed flames ten metres long. It pounded the ground with its huge hooves, and then let out a bellow that turned their blood to water. As the bull charged, Herakles leapt sideways and sprang on to its back. Grabbing hold of its razor-tipped horns, he wrestled the bull to the ground where Iolaus quickly tied it up. Herakles heaved the huge bull on to his shoulders and smiled proudly.

"Let's see what King Eurystheus has to say about this monster," he said.

When the cowardly king saw the bull alive and kicking on Herakles's back, he went MAD.

"AGHHH! Take it away!" he screamed.

Herakles was disappointed.

"Great Zeus! I can't do anything to please you," he said.

"Please stop bringing monsters into my palace," begged the king, and he hid in a cupboard until Herakles had set the bull free.

So ends The Labours of Herakles Part 1.
Read more in Part 2

The Labours of Herakles

Part 2

The fifth labour took Herakles to the far north, to the land of Thrace, ruled over by the warring king, Diomedes. He was a great fighter, with a war chariot that was pulled by four flesh-eating mares, who were fed enemy soldiers for breakfast, lunch and supper. Herakles had to put a stop to that.

Neither Herakles nor Iolaus fancied staying in the palace of Diomedes, as they were worried he might serve them up for dinner! They headed straight for the stables where they found the mares tied up. When they saw the strangers, the horses rattled their chains and snapped their teeth.

Herakles smashed their chains with his club. The mares reared up on their hind legs and galloped out into the yard. The guards came running, but the mares kicked them to death, and then ate them. Still hungry, they jumped the palace walls and trotted into Diomedes's bedroom where they ate him too.

Once they'd eaten their master, they became tame and very friendly. So Herakles took them to Mycenae, but the king didn't like them either.

"I didn't say capture the mares, I said kill them!" yelled Eurystheus.

"But they're nice now," explained Herakles. "Look, they're really friendly."

He gave the horses sugar lumps, and they licked his hands for more.

"Get them out of here!" yelled the king, and jumped into the cupboard, *again*.

So Herakles set the horses free and they neighed joyfully as they galloped off into the mountains of Arcadia.

When the horses were gone, King Eurystheus came out of the cupboard and gave Herakles his sixth labour.

"Your majesty, when will I get a rest?" asked tired Herakles.

"After 12 years of working for me, you can rest all you want," answered the king. "For your sixth labour, I want you to go to Mount Atlas and bring back the golden apples from the gardens of Hesperides. Atlas will tell you where to find them; he's been there for centuries."

A year later, Herakles and Iolaus arrived at Mount Atlas in Africa where poor Atlas stood, holding up the world.

"Ah! My back's killing me!" he groaned.

"Do you know where I can find the golden apples of the gardens of Hesperides?" asked Herakles.

Atlas nodded his head. "My daughters guard them," he replied.

"Do you think they would let me have some?" asked Herakles.

"Yes, but I would have to ask them myself," said Atlas.

"How?" asked Herakles.

"Well ... if you would be so kind as to hold up the world, I could nip down the hill and speak to them," said Atlas.

"All right," said Herakles.

Atlas lifted the world off his big shoulders and stretched. "Ah, that's wonderful!" he sighed, and smiled up to the sun for the first time in 20 years.

"Don't be long," said Herakles.

"I'll be back just as soon as I can," promised Atlas.

But he was gone a long time and the weight of the world pushed down, heavier and heavier, on to Herakles's aching shoulders.

"What if he doesn't come back?" thought Herakles. "I'll be stuck here for ever and ever and ever, with this terrible load on my shoulders."

When Herakles thought he couldn't stand it a minute longer, Atlas came running up the hill with his arms full of golden apples.

"Sorry I was so long, Herakles, but it was wonderful to be free again. Wonderful!"

Sighing sadly, Atlas bent over, and Herakles put the world back on his shoulders.

"Pray for me," cried Atlas, as Herakles left. "Goodbye ..."

By the time Herakles got back to the court of King Eurystheus, he had only six months left to serve.

"Better make this task a quick one," he told the king.

"Your final labour is to go to the underworld and bring back Cerberus, the hound that guards the gates of Hades," King Eurystheus commanded.

So Iolaus and Herakles crossed the River Styx and entered the world of the dead where they found that Hades, the god of the underworld, and his wife, Persephone, were waiting for them.

"You may borrow Cerberus," they said, "on condition you catch him with your bare hands."

"I'll do my best," said Herakles.

Strolling up to the three-headed hound of hell, he grabbed its huge head and squeezed it hard.

"Owwwwww!" howled Cerberus and immediately fell to the ground.

"Since you have caught him with your bare hands, you may take him to King Eurystheus – but bring him back soon," said Persephone.

Cerberus was a good dog. He walked to heel and didn't snap at anybody. But in Mycenae he turned very nasty.

"WOOOF! WOOOF!" he snarled at weedy King Eurystheus. The king jumped right off his throne.

"Praise be to Zeus, your labours are finished!" he shouted at Herakles. "Now, get out of here and never – *ever* – come back!"

"Rufff!" snapped Cerberus, and bit the king's toe just as they were leaving.

"Good boy," laughed Herakles. "I've been wanting to bite him for years!"

Herakles took Cerberus back to Hades, then he went home too. But after all his marvellous adventures, he couldn't settle to a quiet life. He wanted more adventures, so he travelled the world looking for them. Finally, he became a god – not as great a god as his father, Zeus, but a good god and a great hero – Herakles, the strongest man that ever lived.

Theseus and the Minotaur

When the great hero, Theseus, was born, his father, Aegeus, did a very odd thing. He left him and went away to Athens where he became king.

"When my son grows up," said Aegeus before he left, "give him these gifts."

He ordered six of his soldiers to lift an enormous boulder and put a sword and a pair of sandals underneath it.

"That's not fair!" cried Theseus's mother. "How will anybody be able to lift that boulder again?"

"My son will," said Aegeus. "Tell him to visit me in Athens, carrying the sword and wearing the sandals, then I will know who he is."

Aegeus was right about Theseus – the boy did grow up to be amazingly strong. He could throw a discus, wrestle and run better than any other boy in the city. By the time he was a young man, Theseus was restless. He didn't want to stay at home with his mother; he wanted adventures.

"I must leave and visit my father in Athens," he said one day.

"I know," said his mother sadly. "Take your father's gifts with you."

"Gifts, what gifts?" asked Theseus.

"I will show you," said his mother.

She took Theseus to the boulder and pointed at it.

"Your father left them under there," she said.

"Mother, are you joking?" laughed Theseus.

"No. Your father said you would lift the boulder if you were his son."

"Well, there's no doubt about that!" said Theseus.

He rubbed his hands, took a deep breath and grabbed hold of the enormous boulder.

"Ha-hhh!" he cried, and lifted it.

Underneath, were the sandals and the sword his father had left for him.

"Take them and wear them in Athens," said his mother. "Your father will know who you are and welcome you."

Weeping, she kissed her son goodbye and prayed to the gods to protect him.

When Theseus got to Athens, Medea the witch was waiting for him. She had told King Aegeus that the handsome stranger was an enemy soldier who would try to kill him.

"He must be destroyed," she cried, "before he destroys you and your kingdom!"

"Yes!" cried Aegeus. "I'll kill him with my own sword."

"Leave the killing to me," smiled Medea. "Watch ..."

She mixed poison with wine and poured it into a beaker.

"This is for the stranger!" she cackled. "Ha, ha, ha!"

When Theseus came to the palace, Medea gave him the drink.

"Welcome, stranger," she smiled.

"Your health!" said Theseus. He was just about to gulp back the poison when King Aegeus saw his sandals.

"NO-OOOOO!" he yelled, and smashed the beaker to the ground. "Witch! This is my son, Theseus. You tried to kill him! Get out and never come back!"

"I put a curse on you, Aegeus!" she screamed.

"OUT!" yelled the king. "Before I have you thrown out, in little pieces."

Medea ran away to another country in the far north where, luckily, nobody has ever seen her since. But her curse stayed with Aegeus ... as you will soon learn.

Theseus and the king were happy together, but only for a short time. Every nine years, the king of Athens had to send seven of his strongest boys and seven of his loveliest girls to Crete, to King Minos, who forced them to dance before the giant bull, the minotaur. It was a dance to the death, for no matter how quick and brave they were, the bull always killed the dancers, spearing them on his horns, and then eating them alive.

The bull was the same Cretan bull that Herakles had captured years before. It had escaped from Mycenae and returned to Crete, where King Minos had asked his cleverest inventor to build a prison for it.

"Something really complicated: a prison that nobody can get in or out of – especially the bull!"

Daedalus, the inventor, had thought about the problem for a long time, and then came up with a brilliant idea.

"A maze," he explained to the king. "Circles within circles within circles, with the minotaur in the middle!"

"Amazing! Ha, ha! That's a joke – a-mazing!" laughed King Minos.

Daedalus smiled politely – the king was famous for his rotten jokes. Anyway, he built the maze and put the bull in the middle. There it lived off human flesh – boys and girls who danced to their death.

When Theseus heard about the minotaur, he cried, "*I'll* go to Crete this year!"

"YOU!" exploded the king. "You're my son, I won't let you be killed by a raging bull."

"He won't kill me!" laughed Theseus. "I'll kill *him*!"

He joined the girls and boys on the ship, and the black sails were unfurled.

"We'll be back!" called Theseus, to the crowd waving them off at the harbour. "And when we return, our sails will be white. Remember that, Father. If the minotaur kills me, the sails will be black, but look for white sails – I'm going to sort out this minotaur once and for all! Farewell!"

The ship lifted on the waves and sailed quickly out of the harbour, its black sails gloomy against the sparkling blue sea. The girls and boys on board wept and wept, but Theseus promised he'd save all of them – or die trying.

When they reached Crete, Theseus went straight to the palace at Knossos and asked to speak to King Minos.

"I'm Theseus," he said. "I've come to kill the minotaur!"

King Minos nearly fell off his throne, for never had so brave a hero stood before him. His beautiful daughter, Ariadne, immediately fell in love with the young man from Athens.

"I won't let this one be killed by the minotaur," she decided, and hurried off to talk to Daedalus, the inventor.

"I want you to help me save Theseus, and the other Athenian boys and girls, from the bull," she said.

Daedalus shook his head. "Your father will kill me," he said.

Tears filled Ariadne's eyes. "Please, please, please, p-l-e-a-s-e!" she begged.

Daedalus sighed. "All right, but only on condition that you never tell anybody that I helped you – promise?"

"Promise!" said Ariadne.

"Theseus's life will depend on this!"

He handed Ariadne a big ball of string. "He must tie the end of the string to the gate, at the start of the maze. The string will unroll as he walks along and will guide him back – if he's still alive!"

That's brilliant!

"That's brilliant!" cried Ariadne.

"To kill the minotaur, Theseus must rip one of its horns from its head and stab the monster with it, right between the eyes."

Ariadne went white as a sheet. "That's impossible," she gasped.

"Believe me, it's the only thing that will kill the bull," said Daedalus. "Now, off you go, and don't tell a soul about our meeting."

Ariadne hurried away and found Theseus.
"I will save you, hero, if you'll take me back to
Athens and marry me," she said.

"Yes!" said Theseus, who thought Ariadne was
the prettiest girl he'd ever seen.

Ariadne smiled. "This is what you must do ..."

The next day, Theseus went to the maze.

"Wait for me here," he told the other boys and
girls. "If I'm not back in an hour, you're next."

With tears in their eyes, they watched him
disappear into the dark winding circles of the
labyrinth.

"Goodbye, Theseus," they called. "Good luck!"

Unravelling the ball of string, Theseus walked
on ... and on ... It got darker and spookier as he
turned corner, after corner, after corner. Suddenly,
Theseus stopped dead in his tracks. He could hear
a terrible, blood-chilling roaring.

"Zeus, ruler of the skies, help me," he prayed.

Another noise burst through the labyrinth, a noise so loud it made his hair stand on end – the thundering of hooves so big the ground trembled beneath his feet. Theseus turned his head this way and that, trying to guess which way the minotaur would come at him. With a roar, it thrashed through the centre of the maze and stood glaring at Theseus, its nostrils blazing fire, its head bent, its horns as sharp as razors and gleaming white.

Theseus stood and stood and stood, until he could feel the monster's blazing nostrils scorching his toes – then he jumped. With amazing strength and bravery, he leapt right between the minotaur's horns and landed on its back. Theseus held on, balancing on the minotaur's back like a dancer.

The bull tossed its head, trying to throw him up and spear him on its huge horns, but Theseus held on to his horns and gripped them tighter and tighter and tighter. Suddenly, he yanked one of the horns clean out of the bull's head, then leapt through the air and landed in front of the minotaur.

"Dance with me!" he laughed.

Dripping blood, the crazy bull pawed the ground, and then charged. It came at Theseus once more, but he didn't move, he didn't even tremble. Lifting the horn like a javelin, he threw it with all his might. His aim was spot on. The horn hit the minotaur right between the eyes and it fell to the ground, howling in pain.

Grabbing the horn, Theseus ran back through
the labyrinth, following the string's every twist
and turn.

His friends couldn't believe their eyes when
he burst out, his fist held tight in victory.

"I killed it!" he cried. "Now, let's get out
of here!"

With the Cretan army chasing them like
bloodhounds, Theseus and his friends raced to the
harbour where Ariadne was waiting for them on
board the ship.

"Set sail!" she yelled, and with the wind puffing
out their black sails, they whisked across the
dancing sea, singing and laughing.

Theseus was so happy he forgot all about the sails, so instead of changing them to white they stayed black.

When his father saw them blowing against the blue sky, he cried out in agony, "Ahhhhh! My son is dead!"

Medea's wicked curse had come true. Aegeus threw himself off the cliffs, and from that day to this, the sea in which Aegeus drowned has been called the Aegean Sea, in memory of him.

Theseus's journey had come to an end. He became a great king of Athens, but he never did marry the beautiful Ariadne. Dionysus, the god of wine, took her away to live with him on Mount Olympus. Theseus was wise enough to know that a mortal – even a great hero – never challenges the gods!

Daedalus and Icarus

When the minotaur was killed by Theseus, King Minos knew exactly who was to blame.

"Daedalus!" he yelled. "You told Theseus the way out of the maze!"

"Not quite, your majesty. I told your daughter and *she* told him."

"Hah!" shouted Minos, who would have liked to kill Daedalus right there and then, but he didn't. (A live inventor is better than a dead one, especially when he's a brilliant one.)

"You can live, but you're not going to enjoy yourself," snapped Minos. "I'm going to lock you in the maze and throw away the key."

Daedalus, with all his tools and his workbench, was taken to the maze by soldiers.

"You won't get out of here in a hurry," they laughed, "not unless you can fly!"

But the inventor had a plan of escape so brilliantly clever, nobody could ever have guessed it.

"King Minos, before you lock me away, will you allow me one last favour?" he asked.

"What?" asked the king.

"Can my son, Icarus, come with me?"

"No!" answered the king. "This isn't a party, this is prison."

"But, your majesty, I can't work on my own. I need somebody to help me invent things, somebody young and strong, like my son," coaxed Daedalus.

"Hum, all right then," agreed the king. "But he'd better work hard – you too!"

As soon as he was alone with his son, Daedalus grabbed hold of him and hugged him.

"Oh, Icarus!" he cried. "We're going to get out of here, together!"

Icarus looked at the maze and the heavy metal gates blocking the entrance.

"Out," he gasped. "How?"

Daedalus smiled. "We're going to fly," he cried and started to run round the maze, flapping his arms and laughing, "Wheeeeee!"

Icarus thought his father had gone mad.

"Stop it, Father, we're not birds," he said. "How can you expect us to fly?"

"Because I'm going to make a flying machine," answered Daedalus, "and you're going to help me."

In secret they set to work. To start with, they built two light, wooden frames.

"We'll strap them around us like this," said Daedalus, fastening a frame on to his chest, "and then we'll stick feathers on with wax."

"Feathers?" cried Icarus. "Where do we get feathers in this maze?"

"We get them from up there," said Daedalus, nodding at two huge golden eagles circling the sky above the labyrinth. "We shoot them."

Luckily Icarus was a good shot with his catapult. The birds fell to the ground, and Icarus plucked out their feathers.

"Put each feather into the hot wax ... like this," Daedalus said.

Icarus watched his father and did the same. They stuck all the feathers on to the frames and left them to dry for a week. Then they strapped their flying frames on to their chests, and flapped their wings.

"How does it feel?" asked Daedalus.

"Wonderful!" smiled Icarus. "Let's go right now, Father."

"No, wait till morning," said Daedalus. "We'll leave at dawn, when the guards are sleepy."

When the sun came up, Daedalus and his son strapped on their golden wings.

"Here we go!" cried Daedalus.

"One, two, three – and away!"

Up they went, high into the blue, blue sky.

"Look at me, Father!" shouted Icarus. "I'm a bird – I can fly!"

He was so excited, he flew higher and faster than Daedalus, dipping and diving like a swallow.

"Be careful!" called his father. "Don't go too near the sun, or it will melt your wings."

Icarus didn't hear him. "Wheee!" he cried, as he zipped through a cloud and zoomed high into the sky. "Father, you're a genius!"

As Icarus flew nearer and nearer to the sun, Daedalus could see the wax on his wings start to bubble and boil.

"NO! NO!" screamed Daedalus. "The sun!"

Too late. Icarus was falling, tumbling and turning. He reached out his hands and cried for help. "Father, save me!"

There wasn't a thing Daedalus could do. With a terrible cry, Icarus fell into the sea – the Icarian Sea, named in memory of him, the first boy ever to fly like a bird.

Our HERO Comes Home!

An exclusive interview with handsome hunk Herakles, by our Junior Reporter, Damian, for *Hot!* magazine

JRD: Where does your great strength come from?

H: From my dad's side of the family. He's Zeus, the most powerful of the Greek gods. I get my good looks from Mum!

me and my amazing father outside his weekend cottage

JRD: Were you scared when you first saw the lion of Nemea?

H: Nah! He was a pussycat … had him eating out of my hand.

JRD: What gave you the idea to singe the stumps from the hydra's heads?

H: Well, I had to ask a friend to help on that one. I'm strong, but people tell me I lack a little in the brains department. Iolaus, my servant, thought of the burning idea. Credit where credit is due.

JRD: What did you make of the Cretan bull?

H: Yeah, well, he was really terrifying. He was breathing fire, remember? And when I jumped on his back, he kept trying to throw me off. And hauling that heavy weight to the king wasn't much fun … I got a bit out of breath there.

JRD: You were almost fooled by Atlas, weren't you? He nearly left you carrying the can!!

H: No way, I knew he'd come back. He likes having the weight of the world on his shoulders. It makes him feel important.

JRD: Was your trip to Hades exciting? All that doomy, gloomy stuff?

H: That was really cool ... literally. And damp too. But the dog, Cerberus, was cute, I'll get a pet when I stop travelling.

fun with Cerberus

JRD: What was your worst labour?

H: Those stinking stables – phew, I hate pongs more than anything.

JRD: And your favourite?

H: Hmmmm ... I think I'd have to say getting those golden apples. Atlas's daughters were really fit.

Here at Hot! we think Herakles is so brave and strong!

Ideas for reading

Written by Clare Dowdall BA(Ed), MA(Ed)
Lecturer and Primary Literacy Consultant

Learning objectives: compare different types of narrative and information texts and identify how they are structured; infer writers' perspectives from what is written and what is implied; explore how writers use language for comic and dramatic effects; use and explore different question types

Interest words: labours, mortal, oracle, arrowhead, marathon, hydra, minotaur, Hades, underworld, Cerberus

Resources: question cards: Who? What? Why? Where? When? How?, picture of the hydra and the minotaur

Curriculum links: History: Who were the Ancient Greeks?, How do we use Ancient Greek ideas today?

Getting started

This book can be read over two or more guided reading sessions.

- Read the title and blurb on the front and back covers. Ask if anyone knows any characters from the Greek myths. Introduce the hydra and the minotaur as examples.

- Discuss and explain what the word "myth" means.

- Read the contents together. Model and remind children to use a range of strategies to read new and tricky words.

- Explain that you are going to read about the labours of Herakles. Ask children to predict what a "labour" might be.

Reading and responding

- Read pp2-3 to the children. Discuss the tone of the narrative voice. Is it funny or serious? Formal or informal? Approving or disapproving of Herakles? Ask children to give reasons for their ideas.

- In pairs, ask children to read to p10 to find out how Herakles defeats the lion of Nemea. Discuss the narrative voice and ask for examples of humour and dramatic language.